I0804438

The Ghostly Tales of Southwest Pennsylvania

Published by Arcadia Children's Books
A Division of Arcadia Publishing
Charleston, SC
www.arcadiapublishing.com

Copyright ©2022 by Arcadia Children's Books
All rights reserved

Spooky America is a trademark of Arcadia Publishing, Inc.

First published 2022

Manufactured in the United States

ISBN 978-1-4671-9881-3

Library of Congress Control Number: 2022933033

All images courtesy of Shutterstock.com.

Notice: The information in this book is true and complete to the best of our knowledge. It is offered without guarantee on the part of the author or Arcadia Publishing. The author and Arcadia Publishing disclaim all liability in connection with the use of this book.

All rights reserved. No part of this book may be reproduced or transmitted in any form whatsoever without prior written permission from the publisher except in the case of brief quotations embodied in critical articles and reviews.

Spooky America

The Ghostly Tales of Southwest Pennsylvania

Karen Emily Miller

dapted from *Ghosts of Southwestern Pennsylvania* by Thomas White

arcadia
CHILDREN'S BOOKS

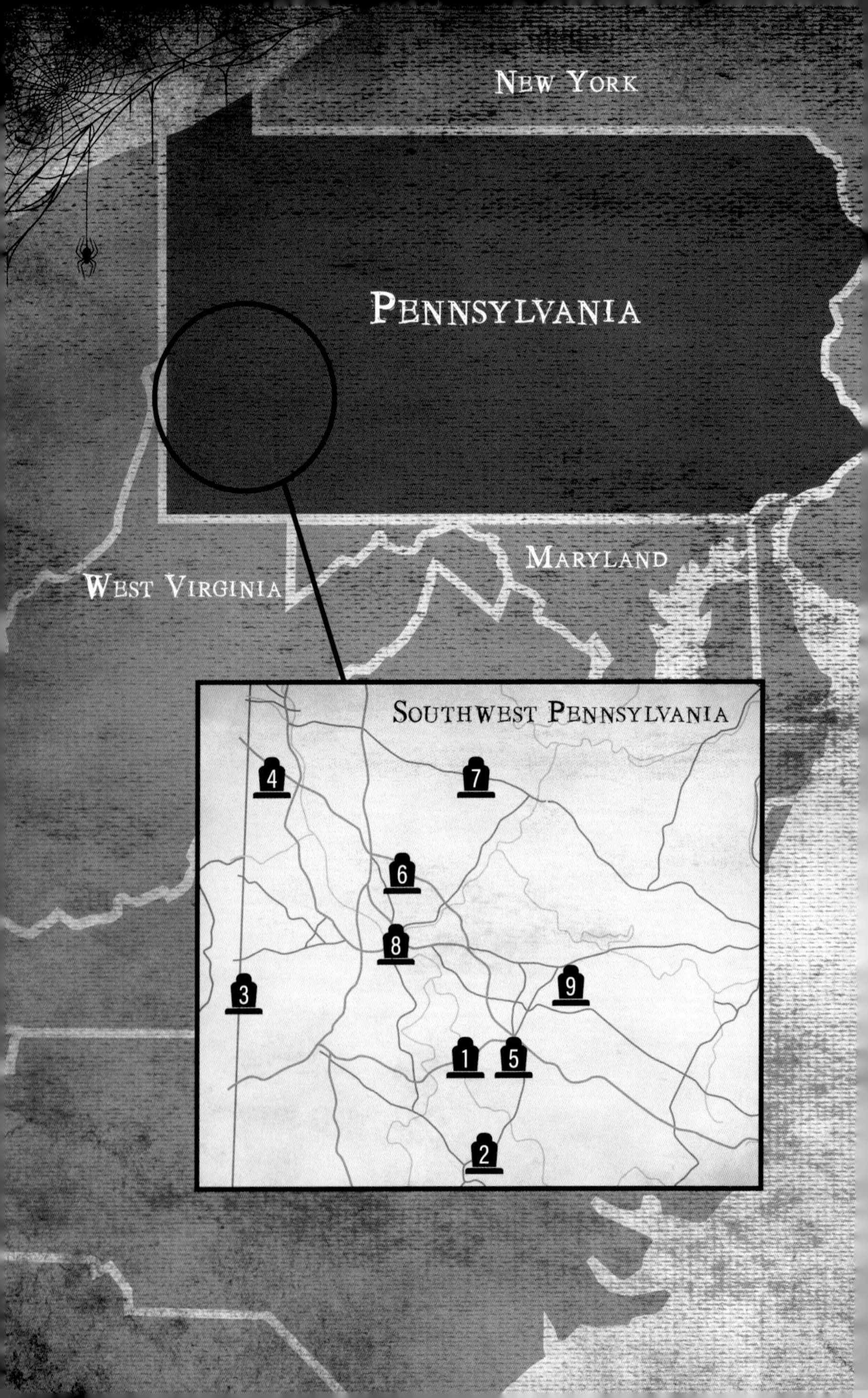
New York
Pennsylvania
Maryland
West Virginia
Southwest Pennsylvania
4
7
6
8
3
9
1
5
2

Table of Contents & Map Key

Introduction

Road trip! Get in the family car and settle in with soft plushy blankets. You have a week or two to discover why people say Southwestern Pennsylvania is so special. You've always wanted to visit an Amish farm. How do people live without electricity and cars? You'd like to ride the funicular that soars up the side of Mount Washington. Wooden cable cars, incredible views of Pittsburgh, and tasty goodies? That's a trip you'd like to take.

That's not all. Southwest Pennsylvania has more to offer. Besides thrills and discoveries, there are ghosts to find. There's Deacon, who only wants to help, and picky Mrs. Bruhns, who doesn't approve of changes to her haunted room. The cranky spirits of West Overton village might scold you, but don't let that stop you. And that is just the beginning.

Ok, click your seat belt. Let's go!

CHAPTER 1

Ghostly Graves

Have you been to a cemetery lately? Yes? During the daylight hours? Good for you. Now, let me ask, have you been to a graveyard just before midnight? Have you studied the tombstones just as the clock strikes midnight?

Actually, you don't have to wait until the witching hour to see something spooky at the Hoffman cemetery in Westmoreland County, Pennsylvania. If you visit it anytime it's dark, you'll see a glowing tombstone. Some say you can stand several hundred yards away and still see its light. Strangely, the tombstone's light fades and eventually disappears as you approach it.

But what causes the light? The tombstone itself is made from pink marble, a material not known to glow. Over the years, many have come to the cemetery, trying to solve the mystery of the ghostly glow.

Recently, the mystery might have been solved. Paranormal researchers attached an outside light to a building just over hill from the cemetery. Investigators found that when the light's radiance was blocked and it couldn't send its beams over the crest of the hill, the tombstone did not glow.

Your next stop on the graveyard tour is an abandoned Quaker meeting house. It's in its cemetery that you can find a different mysterious tombstone. This one doesn't glow. It's claim to fame? It puts a curse on all those who reads its inscription aloud.

The Quaker church is a bit disappointing as you and your friends roll up to it on your bikes. The church building is small and needs repairs. On earlier trips, always made in the daylight, you counted the dusty battered pews inside the church. There can't be more than ten. So, you know the building is smaller than most churches. It also needs renovation. That doesn't make it haunted, though, does it?

Still, there's something strange here. Is it the location of the meeting house? Its sits in the middle of the cemetery and is surrounded by a tall, spiky fence. Is the iron fence protecting the church or keeping what's inside the cemetery from escaping ? Either way, you'd hate to get stuck on it if you have to make a quick getaway from specters.

You make a note to yourself that, no matter what, you won't climb the fence. Still, your curiosity pulls you into the yard. You promise yourself that you will discover if the church and its tombstones can hex you.

Even though there is a sign warning against paranormal investigation, you and your friends chuckle and elbow nudge each other. It's time to find the tombstone with the curse.

The librarian in town told you where to find it. "Don't tell anyone I told you," she said, and winked. "And remember, don't step on the grave it marks. That will bring a curse down, too."

The librarian, who noticed nearby adults chuckling, said loudly, “Some of you don’t think the curse is true. Fayette County has had more than its share of tragedies. Just last month a teenager tested the legend by reading the inscription aloud. He had a serious car accident a few days later. Why does it happen here in the county? Is it because our people had more opportunities to touch or read the inscription? It is in our back yard, after all.”

You find the grave. The librarian’s directions were perfect. You and your friends gather around. You wonder if you should remind your friends not to step on the grave or read aloud the words on the tombstone. You read the words to yourself, silently. You even clap your hands over your mouth, just to make sure none of the words escape from your lips.

The inscription doesn't read like a hex. In fact, it reminds you of an anonymous poem your English teacher made you memorize.

"Remember youth as you go by,
As you are now, so once was I.
As I am now so you shall be,
Beware of death and follow me."

You remember thinking the poem was depressing and wondering why your teacher had your class learn it. The reminder that you have only a short time on earth is a bit frightening. Is that why our teachers want us to recall it? Do they want us to be careful with our lives? Are they afraid that, after reading the inscription, we'd think about its meaning instead of paying attention to the road and cars driving on it?

"Don't worry," says one of your friends. "None of us read the whole inscription out loud. We took turns reading different parts."

If they don't worry, you won't either. After all, spooky things have happened to people who never stepped on the grave or read the poem aloud. Last year, a neighbor, who had been driving by the church for years, suddenly slowed his car down to a few miles an hour. He wondered if he could spot the cursed tombstone. Suddenly, a huge black dog leapt in front of his car. The car's headlights showed the dog's glowing eyes. They were phosphorescent, like the yellow brightly colored wrist bands you wear in the

dark. Your neighbor rolled up his car windows as fast as he could. He didn't want that dog inside his car. Still, the low growling rumble seeped inside. Your neighbor stepped on the gas and raced away. According to the librarian, he hasn't gone back there since.

Another driver had a close call when he passed the church. It was night, so maybe that explains why he didn't see the old woman until the last moment.

"She jumped out in front of my car," he said. "I wrenched the wheel so I wouldn't hit her. I skidded off into the bushes. I'm lucky I didn't get hurt myself."

He explained how he had spent hours looking alongside the road for the old woman. Surely, he must have hit her. It had all happened so fast. He couldn't be sure. He never did find her.

That wasn't the last time the old lady was seen. She appears, from time to time, on the road in front the little church. If you slow down and turn your car off, which is a natural thing to do if you see an old woman wandering alone at night, you will be very sorry.

According to those who've experienced it, your car's battery will go dead. When you look into your rearview mirror, you'll see the old lady's face, wrinkled and pale, staring at you with empty eyes.

"Let's get going," one of your friends say. Somewhere a church bell chimes eleven. No one wants to be in a churchyard at midnight. Who knows what could appear at the strike of twelve? You all jump on your bikes and ride past the little church, past the graves, and through the spiky iron gates. You're relieved that you aren't driving in a car. When you look over your shoulder, there's no old woman in the rearview mirror.

CHAPTER 2

Moll Derry, Fortune-teller of the Revolution

What is a witch? Is it someone who can fly? Or is it someone who finds lost objects, animals, even a person or two? Perhaps it's someone who casts spells. Moll Derry was a woman who was said to be a master of all of these.

Moll Derry is no made-up story. She was a real woman who lived in Southwest Pennsylvania in the 1790's. Everyone agreed that Moll was a practitioner of a powerful form of folk magic called hex or powwow. A powwow for Moll and other German healers wasn't a get together with the local Native Americans. It was a trance-like ritual for healing. Powwows didn't rely on magic or enchantments. The German settlers trusted the wisdom of the Bible, too. Most, if not all, of the ceremonies, used the Bible in their rituals.

Powwows were people trained in healing and spells. Some said they had cures for physical afflictions, protections against curses, and that they could put a hex on someone.

Moll was known to be one of the best powwows.

If you lost your grandfather's pocket watch, you'd go to Moll. If you had a wart, you'd call on Moll. And, though you wouldn't share this with anyone, if you wanted to punish the boy who kicked you at recess, you'd visit Moll.

Moll could help you avenge insults and crimes against you. She also was known to be a great avenger for herself. Everyone knew not to cross Moll.

Unfortunately, for three lazy men in town, not everyone believed she had power. One afternoon, three good-for-nothings stopped at the local tavern. They poured down mug after mug of ale and entertained themselves by making jokes about Moll. Moll happened by and heard them.

"Surely, you don't believe your insults."

The men laughed.

"Perhaps, you would like to say you are sorry for saying them?"

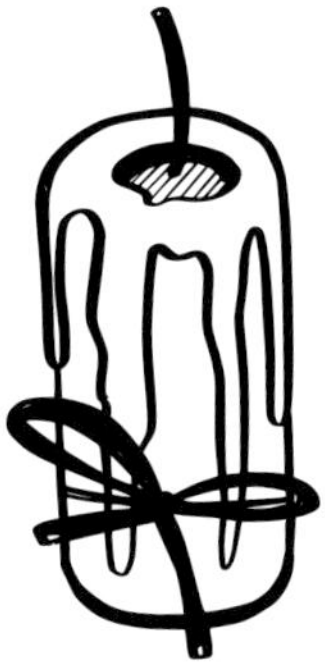

This time the men laughed so hard they snorted. They even spit up a little of the beer.

Moll held up her hand. "Enough!

You three have just cursed yourselves. It will be your words that leave you dangling from a hangman's rope."

Shaking her head, Moll turned and left the tavern.

A few months later, the first of the men to insult Moll got drunk and killed a man. The punishment? Hanging. A few weeks later, the second man murdered someone. He fled and avoided capture. He wasn't as lucky when he killed another man. Then, he was caught, convicted and hanged within days, just as Moll predicted.

It didn't take long for the news to spread. Moll's curse was coming true. The third man thought he could outrun Moll's hex. His life was peaceful, until it wasn't. A few weeks after he settled in a new town, he was also found hanging.

Who knows what changed his fate? Had he seen Moll on the street? Had his rude treatment of Moll become known to the people in the new town? No one knows why.

Moll couldn't abide bad behavior, even when she wasn't the one being injured. A young woman named Polly Williams had the bad luck to be beautiful. Worthless men courted her and promised her a happy life. Polly was wise enough to know that most of them weren't to be trusted. While pretty, Polly came from a poor family. She knew that most young men sought daughters with wealthy parents.

Polly found a position as a maid with a well-to-do family. They treated her well, and Polly thought her luck had changed. When a neighbor, Phillip Rogers, told her she was the wife he wanted, Polly believed him.

Her family decided to move west, hoping

for a better life. Polly, though, stayed. She was certain Phillip would marry her. But when . . . how . . . where? So, when Polly saw Moll, she asked Moll to predict her future.

Moll closed her eyes, and chanted words Polly couldn't understand. Moll swayed back and forth and muttered to herself. When she finished, she opened her eyes. Could that have been a tear rolling down her cheek?

"I see, dear girl, your future. I see your fiancé throwing you off a cliff." Moll put her hands on Polly's shoulders and looked into her eyes. "Break off the engagement. Don't see him again, ever."

Polly, though, now believed her beauty would convince Phillip to marry her. "I cannot believe what you are saying. He would never do such a thing. He loves me!"

Moll shrugged and left Polly behind on the footpath. "Foolish girl," she muttered.

Moll's prediction came true a few months later. Phillip told Polly he had hired a minister to marry them. To make the wedding memorable, he said that they should marry on the cliffs of White Rocks. It had been a meeting place for them while courting.

The story gets fuzzy after Polly left her employer's house that day. The other servants saw her go and wished her well.

When Polly didn't return, a search party began looking for her. The town's minister was asked about the planned ceremony. He said Phillip had never said anything about performing a wedding.

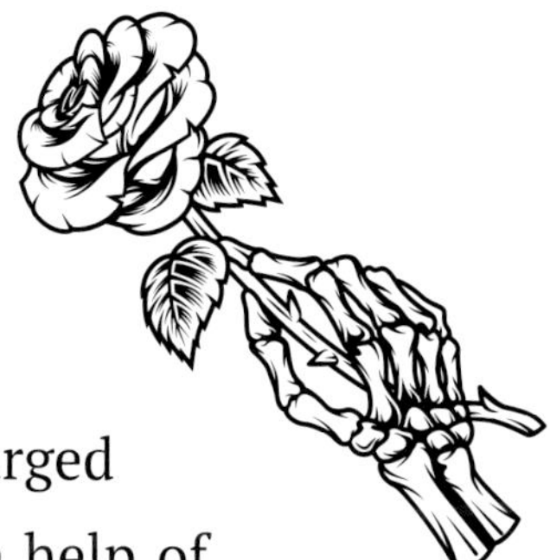

The townspeople found Polly on the white rocks below the cliff. Someone had thrown her off the cliff.

Phillip, of course, was charged with Polly's murder. With the help of expensive counselors, he was able to convince the judge he wasn't guilty.

The townspeople couldn't believe how Phillip Rogers shrugged off any guilt for Polly's death. He lived close to the White Rocks for the rest of his life. He asked to be buried them near them after he died. Did he finally feel responsible for Polly's death? No one knows.

What is known is that there is a specter haunting the cliffs of the White Rocks. It's a woman, oddly similar in shape and size to

Polly. The ghost usually appears when the fog lies heavy on the White Rocks. Is it the ghost of Polly, looking for Phillip?

People say they are waiting for the day when Polly avenges her death. Phillip might be a ghost, but even a ghost is not safe from Moll's avenging spirit. Polly had been wronged. It would be just like Moll to wait until the time is right to punish Phillip. Certainly, waiting a few hundred years to avenge Polly is not impossible for a skilled powwow.

CHAPTER 3

Shades of Death Road

You don't want to be late. You promised your mom you'd pick up your sister at the library before it closes at 7 pm. The problem is this: It's the middle of December and it's dark out. One thing is for certain: you are *not* afraid of the dark. That feeling belongs to little kids. Normally, you enjoy a chance to drive the car by yourself now that you are old enough to. Usually, your little brother or sister ride along and tonight, you wouldn't mind having company. It's the name of this road. What kind of town names a road "Shades of Death?"

You asked your grandfather about it. "I'll give you as many reasons as I can, he answers with a wink. "The first," he says, "was malaria. Some of the early settlers made a poor choice for land. They built their homes on swampy land, and swamps are perfect breeding grounds for mosquitoes. Mosquitoes can carry malaria, and if you're bitten, you can get it. Many of the settlers did and they died by the hundreds."

"Another reason are these towering trees lining the road. These hemlock trees kept the road in perpetual shade. That, and the fact that so many people died, earned the road its gruesome name." He paused and cleared his throat.

"Some people say they see a shadow man lurking around the road. People think the shadow men are the ghosts of the men who were killed alongside of the road."

"That brings me to the final possibility, tragedy. Some say one young man was late going home. He went too fast and lost control of his car. Locals say he swerved because a ghost appeared in front of him. So now, people say, there are two ghosts at the spot. The young

man's spirit must not know he is dead. Perhaps that is why he roams the woods every night."

Your grandfather finishes and you think, all of the reasons could be true. Or all of them false. Knowing this doesn't make you feel any better. Just a few more miles and you'll be in town. You don't realize it, but you are speeding up.

You're thinking about the ghosts when suddenly, kablam, a tire blows. You stop the car. The tire is ruined. There's no way you can drive on that tire all the way to town.

There's only one thing to do. You must change it.

Your heart thuds. You feel a bit light-headed. You can't sit in the car all night; your sister is waiting at the library. You wonder if your pounding heart drowns out the rustling noises from the woods. Your attention is on changing the tire. After you tighten the last lug nut, you sense that someone or something nearby is breathing heavily. Twigs break. Leaves crunch. *Huuh . . . Huuh . . .* What is panting so hard? Out of the corner of your eye you see a shadow.

You jump up and tighten your grip on the wrench. For just a moment, a figure seems to take a step towards you. Then, just as suddenly as it appeared, it vanishes.

You toss the wrench into the trunk, gun the motor and take off. You're careful not to speed, though. Even if the stories aren't true, you don't want to be another foolish fellow that risks his life buy driving too fast on the Shades of Death Road. You definitely don't want to be ghost #3.

CHAPTER 4

The Specter of Summit Cut Bridge

Bridges are built for very good reasons. They link towns and businesses, and most importantly, people. The Summit Cut Bridge was built to reconnect the citizens of Beaver County. The Pennsylvania Railroad had cut ravines through the land so they could lay railroad tracks. The railroad was a boon, but it also cut through roads used for hundreds of years. The locals were thrilled when the

110-foot wooden bridge was finished and the county was reconnected.

However, people say, that life-connecting bridge was no bargain. Accidents, one after another, began piling up. Even though the original wooden bridge has been replaced by one made of steel and concrete, it still has troubles.

It's fairly new, built in the 1970s. However, the average life of a bridge is fifty years. After that, more maintenance needs to be done.

Repairs aren't the only problems the Summit Cut Bridge has. It has serious haunting troubles. Some people say there's a curse, too, born the night a young woman crashed through the guardrail.

She had been driving home in a torrential rainstorm. She took the route she always did, over the Summit Cut Bridge. Had she been driving too fast for road conditions? Had something jumped in front of her car? Or had the guardrail, fifty years old, simply collapsed when the car hit it? No one knows.

The only fact people can agree on is that the young woman's car went off the bridge. The next morning the searchers found it in a ravine, ninety feet below the bridge. It had crashed into the ravine below, nothing but a crumple of steel on the railroad track.

Ever since that night, accidents have occurred at an alarming rate. Some drivers have reported a ghost under the bridge on rainy nights. They have to squint to see it, but they are certain a woman's shadow is wandering about the accident site. They say she waves her

arms, trying to direct the drivers off the bridge. Some people have seen phantom headlights swerving off the bridge and plunge to the ravine below.

The locals argue that the paranormal activity began long before the young woman skidded off the bridge.

In 1891, a train was rumbling through the ravine when it accidentally hit an old man who had gotten too close to the tracks. Three years later, a woman lost her balance while walking on the bridge. She fell to her death. In 1937, a car crashed through the guard rail cable and plummeted into the ravine. A forty-one-year-old woman drove off the bridge at the same spot seventeen years later.

Then, in 1952, accident occurred that convinced everyone the bridge had to be fixed immediately. A man and woman had traveled only twenty feet onto the bridge when their car began to skid. The car scraped off thirty feet of guardrail before it plunged down over the side.

After that, the state not only widened the bridge from fourteen to twenty feet, it straightened a sharp curve, too.

Have the accidents stopped? Is the female ghost still there? You decide to make an investigation yourself. You check your bike headlights to make sure they shine clear and bright. You don't want to risk getting hit by a car. You have a set of two headlamps, not the usual single bulb most bikes use. You tell yourself that the ghost will be attracted to two lights, for that suggests a car is behind the beams, not a bicycle. Plus, you want to be able to see the ghost, if she's there. Then you wait for a rainy night. That's when most of the accidents happened. Paranormal researchers say it's helpful to match the same conditions as when the spirit last appeared.

You're not afraid when you ride onto the bridge. It doesn't look frightening at all. In fact, it looks very safe. So, why is your heart thumping? It's pounding so fast you are surprised your rain slicker doesn't move out and in with the force of your heartbeats. You shiver. It was warm when you left the house. Now it's cold, almost as if a winter storm front has blown in. You feel the presence of someone else.

Positioning your bike this way and that, you hope the beams will illuminate whatever might be on the bridge with you. Then you see her. It's a woman. Her skirt flows around her, almost as if she were being buffeted by wind. She wheels one arm up and around and points down with the arm. Is she signaling that someone below the bridge needs help? You came to see a ghost, but you're not going to ignore someone who might be in danger. You slowly ride closer to the spirit. She circles her arm again, points to the ravine below. You lean your bike against the guard wall and peer over. Nothing is there. When you look up again, you see that the ghost is within a few feet you. The ribbons of shadows cover most of her face, you can't even see her eyes. But what you do see makes you jump on your bike and race home. The spirit was smiling at you.

CHAPTER 5

West Overton

You lag behind your classmates as they file off the school bus. You're about to spend an afternoon at the historic town that had been built around the distilling of whiskey. It's called Overton. The local historic society restored or recreated the eighteen buildings that made up the heart of the village. You're armed with a list of questions you must answer for your teacher after the tour. Boring!

Little do you know that you're about to have one of the most exciting afternoons of your life.

The teacher introduces your class to a guide. He's tall, skinny and wears an old-fashioned hat. He must want to look like one of the first settlers, you think.

The guide clears his throat like people do when they are about to give a speech. "Many of these buildings existed when Overton was a booming town. Many visitors, immigrants and settlers passed through. Some of them, people say, never left." The guide arches his eyebrows as you make your first stop on the tour. "It doesn't look haunted, does it?"

You perk up. Could the guide be talking about the house in front of you? It's a cheerful red brick home, three stories tall with a front porch so inviting it looks as if you could spend an afternoon rocking on a porch swing. What could be scary about that?

The guide talks in a low voice.

You have to strain to hear him.

"It happened on the third floor of the house. That's where forty-five-year-old Clyde Overholt died. His mother had died three months before. People wondered if it was grief that killed him."

"Let's go there," you pipe up.

"Unfortunately, the third floor is off limits to visitors. But I'll tell you everything I've seen and heard since I've worked here."

The guide leads the class to the front staircase. "We've all have heard footsteps going up, going down." He thumps his foot on the first step and makes everyone jump. "But when anyone looks, nothing and no one is there."

Suddenly, the guide points to the top of the stairs. "Look, everyone, before it disappears!"

Is this a trick to scare schoolkids? When you look to the top of the stairs you see something dressed like woman. She's wearing a filmy white dress. She's not another guide. When she moves, her silhouette flutters and trembles.

The guide pulls a handkerchief from his pocket and wipes his forehead. He seems as startled as the rest of you.

"You'd think I'd be accustomed to seeing ghosts by now. All of us on staff have."

Somewhere in the house a phone rings and rings. Finally, the noise stops.

The guide laughs, the kind of laugh that's more nervous than happy. "Sometimes we hear a phone ring, but the ringing doesn't come from any of the phones in the museum.

We can't explain it. We hear it, but we can't find it."

You pull out your phone. The next time you see a ghost, you're going to take a picture of it. This is exciting!

"You might want to put that phone back in your pocket," the guide says. "Last month a camera was yanked away from a visitor and slammed to the

floor. All we saw was the camera flying out of the man's hand, levitate for a moment, then crash down at the man's feet."

You put your phone back in your pocket.

That was interesting, you think as the guide leads your class to the outside.

Your next stop is the town store, called the West Overton Emporium.

"If you're hungry, you'll find treats," he says. "Or, if you want to buy a souvenir, you'll find lots of choices. Our best seller is a patch of the two-headed cow named Jasper."

A two headed cow? Now, that's something you wouldn't forget.

The guide laughs that nervous laugh again. "If you're lucky, or unlucky, you'll see the shadow man."

You wonder why he keeps working here if he's so scared. You can't wait to see what's next.

At the back of the store is a narrow staircase. You're told it leads to storage, nothing more. At first, you think it's the guide standing at the top. You wonder, how did he climb the stairs so quickly? After your second look, you see he's not the guide.

He's the shadow man. His shadows, though, aren't the filmy gauzy shapes that you see on a sunny day. The shadows look like they'd ensnare you, like a spider's web might.

The back of your neck prickles. When you look down at your arms, you see the hair standing. Sometimes your body warns you of danger, even before your brain makes sense of what you see, hear, and feel.

The back of your neck won't stop prickling. There are ghosts everywhere! A movement in a corner, a figure you see from the corner of your eye, patches of cold you must walk through, they're all signs that something strange happens here. You decide not to visit the distillery, where the Overton family made rye whiskey. You hear that one of the workers was told to "get out." It wasn't a whispered suggestion. It was an angry order. The voice was so fierce that the distillery worker ran!

When paranormal researchers stayed overnight on an investigation, they reported a rocking chair roll forward, roll back. The lights in the museums turned off again and again, even though no one touched the light switch.

You're glad you'll be gone before it gets dark out. Let someone else see the red and yellow lights that burn by the ovens where coal was made into coke.

You do have time to make one more stop. It's the boyhood home of Henry Clay Frick, a steel baron. He was one of the richest men in America in the late 1800s. How scary could a rich kid's ghost be?

You've just stepped over the threshold to the house when your neck prickles and your hair stands up.

"What are you doing in my house?" A deep voice crackles. You're surprised that no one else hears.

"What are you doing in my house?" The voice booms.

"I'm not in your house," you say as you back out the door. "Not anymore."

You don't wait to hear the voice answer. You run past the other kids and are the first one on the bus. Claiming a seat in the back, you peek

out the rear window. Nothing there but your teacher and your classmates. You notice some of them are running. Some are glancing behind themselves. Even your teacher looks odd. She leans out the bus door, looks around, then slams it shut. "Go!" she says to the bus driver.

No one is sleeping, like they usually do, as the bus makes it way back to school. You don't either. You promise yourself that next time your neck prickles, look left, look right and don't make any sudden moves. If your hair stands up, run the other way.

CHAPTER 7

Depreciation Lands Museum

If someone told you you'd find ghosts at a place called Depreciation Lands Museum, you might laugh. What kind of a museum would call its Depreciation Lands? What are the Depreciation Lands?

It's an awkward name for a generous act by the young American government. The soldiers who fought in the Revolutionary War had been paid in continental currency, depreciated money that had lost most of its value after the war. The leaders of America wanted to reward the soldiers who had risked their lives for their new country. How could the soldiers be rewarded?

America was young. It didn't yet have a stable currency, but it did have land—700,000 acres of it. And land is what they offered the soldiers. Many of the men decided to accept the gift. The government didn't mention that Native Americans were already living there.

In 1785, families moved to southwest Pennsylvania to start a new life. Soon settlements sprang up, with churches, schoolhouses, blacksmith shops, even wagon houses. The immigration took hold and prospered.

The resident ghost didn't show

up for almost 100 years. That's when the local historical society decided it was time to repair and renovate the old buildings at the museum.

Paranormal investigators believe spirits attached to the old buildings are awakened by changes. Tearing down walls and digging up foundations disturb the resident spirits who've been resting for many years.

That's what happened one day when a young volunteer teetered on the top of a ladder over a basement stairwell. The boy had been repainting a door frame and was almost finished with the job. Had he tired in the afternoon heat? Had he leaned over to paint one too many times and lost his balance? Or did he lose focus because he saw something unexpected? Whatever the reason, the boy was headed to a fall down the basement steps.

The other workers watched helplessly as the ladder leaned further and further. Surely the boy was going to fall headfirst to his death or terrible injury.

To this day, the workers agree that what they saw made no sense, no sense at all. Suddenly, the ladder switched course and righted itself. The boy half-slid, half-fell down the ladder to the floor. No one blamed him when he said he was finished painting for the day.

Workers gave the nickname "Deacon," to the spirit because he often materialized in the old church. On that afternoon, he began caring for all museum visitors and workers.

Deacon was kept busy during the repairs. A

woman had spent all day trying to make a new window fit into an old frame. She shaved the trim with a knife over and over again. Finally, tired and frustrated, she declared herself "done." She collapsed on a chair nearby, announcing she was taking a break. She said she'd give it one more try . . . later, not now.

That's when she saw Deacon. She hadn't formally met him before this. She told bystanders that she saw a tall skinny man materialize by the window. He was there, and then he wasn't. Now she knew she must have been working too hard. She was imagining things! Then, out of the corner of her eye, she caught of glimpse of old-fashioned boot and homemade woolen pants.

She stood up, trimming knife in hand, and yelled. "Enough is enough. Don't just stand there. Now that you've scared me, the least you can do is give me some help."

No one is sure what happened next. While everyone could see that she still held onto the knife, did she push it down into the frame, or was it the Deacon who guided her hand? Whoever was responsible, everyone agreed, he or she did a good job. The window fit perfectly.

Deacon wasn't finished helping. Restoring an old church is hard work. Fixing walls, evening out floors and updating lighting wears out a person. A worker, after scraping paint off church wall, needed fresh air. She looked out the window, deciding which shady spot would be best for a rest. That's when she saw an old man looking at her through the window. He wore a long dark coat, something too hot to wear on a summer afternoon. *Odd,* she thought to herself, *but not frightening.* Maybe she'd ask him why he wore the coat if she saw him outside.

She finished scraping the wall and went outside. There was a perfect place to sit, right behind a tombstone. As she settled herself in the shade, she sighed. "Aahh . . . peace . . . quiet . . . perfect."

Then a hand touched her shoulder. She yanked away her arm and jumped to her feet.

No one was there!

"What do you want?" She called. No answer. Shrugging, she straightened her skirt and prepared to sit down again.

But what was that, wriggling out of the bushes? A snake! If she hadn't pulled away her arm, her hand would have been in the path of the slithering snake. She was so shaken, she couldn't recall its markings or head shape. There aren't too many venomous snakes in Southwest Pennsylvania, but it takes just one to bite you!

The woman recalls feeling grateful to Deacon, for he's the ghost most likely to have helped her.

After that, the repairs were finished and the museum open to the public. Deacon, perhaps, satisfied that all was well, wasn't seen for years.

Even during this quiet time, Deacon and other spirits made themselves known to the staff. They reported walking through cold spots and hearing mumbles of words. The sound was loud enough to determine that there were real words being spoken, but not loud enough to understand what they meant.

In 1993, Deacon was called to help again. A troop of Girl Scouts had camped out in the building next to the church. It was a fun, busy night until, finally, everyone was ready to go to bed. The leaders and other adults moved to a different room, probably to distance themselves from the girls' all-night giggling and chatting. Sometime during the night, parts of the ceiling collapsed. Old ceiling tiles and light fixtures crashed to the floor. The sleeping

girls, spreading from corner to corner on the floor, should have been injured by the debris. The adults woke at the sound of the first crash. By the time they got to the room, the glass, ceiling tiles and metal lay scattered on the floor. But not one piece of it had touched any of the Girl Scouts.

That's the perfect place for a haunting, you think. If you see a ghost, it will be there to help you, not hurt you. Next time your class has to go on a field trip, you'll tell your teacher Depreciations Lands Museum is first on your list.

CHAPTER 8

Cries at the Black Cross

You've been challenged to spend the night at the Black Cross grave. If you don't, everyone at school will call you a loser.

Graveyards are spooky places. Crops of headstones spread out from one end to the other. Sometimes there are sunken graves. You could trip and land, face first, on top of the person buried below. You know, of course, there would be dirt between you and the corpse. Still, it's creepy!

So why are you afraid of an empty clearing? That's because this one holds hundreds of bodies in just a few graves. Not one body per grave . . . up to twenty bodies piled on top of one another.

How did this happen? People in America don't usually have mass graves. They have rituals that celebrate the dead and lay them to rest—individually. These funerals honor the culture and traditions of the people who died and those who loved them.

What could have happened here in West Winfield Township to allow people to be buried so shamefully?

It started with the Spanish Flu. In September 1918, the flu crept into western Pennsylvania. At first, there were only a few cases. But by October, the flu had infected every community.

Usually, a flu claims its victims from among the very young and the very old. That's because their immune systems, or the body's resistance to infection, isn't as strong as those of the young and middle aged. This flu, though, was different. It triggered the immune system into overdrive, causing organ failure and death. Everyone was in danger from the Spanish influenza.

One place the flu hit particularly hard was in Butler County. This was the destination of hundreds of immigrants from Poland and Slovakia.

There were jobs to be found here. There was a limestone mine, a sand plant, brickyard, salt works, and a tile works. You didn't need to speak English well, you just needed to work hard for your bosses. The immigrants crammed themselves into places to sleep and eat, saving every penny so they could send it home to their families. Because of these close conditions, the flu spread quickly.

Many of the immigrants died. What made the tragedy worse was what happened to them afterwards. There was no family to arrange funerals, no family to mourn them, no family to remember and celebrate their lives.

The owners of the mines and businesses didn't know what to do. If they didn't bury the dead, the flu would spread even more. A local farmer took pity on the dead and the local business owners. He had a place to bury them, an empty field on his farm.

At first, the dead were to be limited to five per grave. But, as the flu peaked in November of 1918, as many as twenty bodies were lowered into one grave. In total, at least three hundred people died in this part of Butler County.

A Catholic priest from nearby Coylesville thought the immigrants deserved better than this. Slowly, but determinedly, he held proper services for all. Finally, after the last flu victim had been buried with dignity, he erected a large black wooden cross at the burial site. This last act of kindness would commemorate the lives lost.

However, the dead could not rest. Was it because they were far from family and home? No one knows. What is certain is that the living said they heard the dead at the Black Cross Cemetery.

In the Northern hemisphere, many of our rituals come to be because the earth seems to go sleep in the fall. Leaves fall, and plants and flowers wither. It seems to be a time where the barrier between the living and dead is very thin. Reports of ghostly visits multiply in the months of October and November. That's when people celebrate Day of the Dead, All Saints Day, and All Souls Day. This belief, along with the fact that most of the immigrants died during October and November, might explain why there are so many reports of the dead communicating with the living at the Black Cross Cemetery.

So, here you are, walking into the glade where almost three hundred people are buried. You are glad it isn't a full moon. People say that's when they hear babies cry beneath the ground. You can't help but shiver when you think about that.

You're also relieved when you see the marker at the site. Once, the black cross towered over the space. But over the years, weather and a few vandals destroyed the wooden cross. In its place stands a white metal sign. It tells the story of those who died. You hope the ghosts of the immigrants will become confused when they cannot find the black cross. Maybe they'll wander somewhere else, at least for tonight.

It's an unseasonably warm night, not like the usual chilly fall nights you're used to. So, why are you cold? It's almost as if a cloud of freezing air settled upon you. You dart glances into the darkness. You decide that if anything comes out of the trees, you'll throw your flashlight at it and run.

It's cold! You shiver even more when you realize it's not the cold that gives you goosebumps.

It's the ground beneath your feet. It's vibrating with sound. You squat so you can hear the noise more clearly.

Leaning over, you place your ear upon the ground. You shut your eyes so you can concentrate. Do you hear words? They come and go, almost as if people are having a conversation. But you can't make sense of what is being said. The voices are low enough that the meaning is muffled.

Later, you can't remember how long you lay there. Your friend said he found you, passed out, at the grave site. He said he began to worry when you didn't arrive at his house at midnight, the time you two had agreed upon. He said he was sorry for daring you to go the cemetery alone. When the church bells rang at 1 am he knew he had to find you.

"There you were," he said, "flat on the ground. I thought you were dead!"

"Did you see or hear anything?" You ask.

"No, I didn't. Did you?"

You say, "No." He could discover that for himself,

You're glad it's over. You're never going back. It's not that the gravesite seemed threatening. It's that, there at the cemetery, the veil between the living and the dead thinned so much, that, if you opened your eyes, you could see into the next world. You didn't want to be there if it ever happened again.

CHAPTER 9

Ghosts in the Cathedral of Learning

You promised your grandmother you'd go with her to one of her favorite places, No, it's not the zoo. It's not the segueway tour of downtown Pittsburgh. She said she was tired of the zoo and didn't think she could balance on a Segueway.

"It's a building to honor all the immigrants," she says.

"We're not immigrants," you argue.

"We're all immigrants," she answers, "except for the Native Americans. The Monanghelas were here first, then came the Delaware and Pawnee . . . "

"Okay, okay," you say. Sometimes it's better not to argue with a grandma.

You have to admit, The Cathedral of Learning is an impressive building. Over 530 feet tall, it has forty-two stories and over 2,000 rooms. Luckily. Grandma is only interested in the twenty-seven rooms that provide exhibits from the different cultures that settled here in Southwest Pennsylvania.

"Oh, a few of those rooms have ghosts. I even saw one, once."

Now you're interested! You follow Grandma, shuffling in and out of the rooms. You like the African culture room. It has an interesting carved wooden door by an artist from Nigeria.

You wish you could have touched the carvings. The profiled figures looked like the Egyptian people painted on the walls of tombs.

The Chinese culture room has ceiling paintings of dragons. They look nothing like the dragons in the fairy tale books your grandma has read to you. They're more like golden snakes with lion-like heads. They even have horns. You'd spend more time there, but Grandma looks at her watch.

"We'd better hurry. The museum closes in two hours."

She leads you to a room labeled The New England Room, circa 1650. As soon as you walk in, you smell something surprising. The aroma of freshly baked bread wafts around the room. However, It doesn't look like anyone has lit the fireplace in weeks.

"Where does that smell of bread come from?" you ask.

Grandma looks at you, eyebrows raised and asks, "You smell it, too?"

Other visitors speak up.

"I smell it, too."

"I thought there must be a kitchen close by."

The guide smiles and motions us to follow her into a closet in the corner of the room. She must be teasing. How are we all going to fit into a closet?

But it's not a closet. It's an entryway to a set of stairs that lead to a bedroom.

You're first up the stairs. A cradle rocks next to a rope bed. Who set it rocking? No one was in the room before you.

"You're not the first to see it," the guide says, "and you won't be the last." She walks over to the rope bed and straightens the quilts.

"See how the quilt was turned down? Just as if someone was readying the bed for sleep?" She looks at each of us, one by one. "I made the bed just a few minutes ago. Someone or something turned the quilt down . . . again."

She leans over the rope bed. "Take a close look at the pillow."

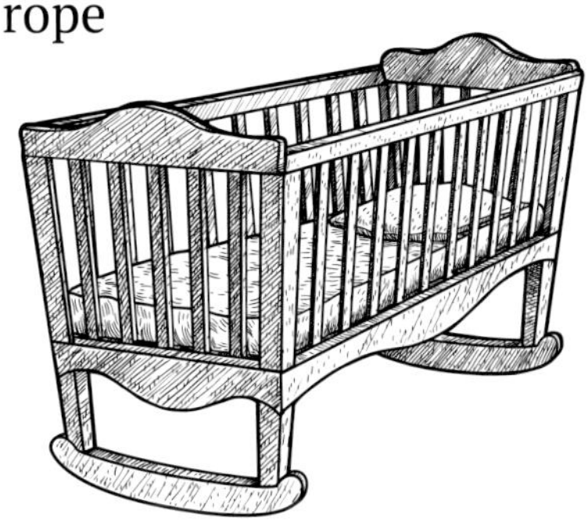

You squint your eyes and concentrate. You can just see the

impression of a head. It looks like your pillow does at home after you've slept on it.

"I'll just fluff it up." The guide says.

Grandma grabs your hand and squeezes it. "Look," she whispers. A shadow is stepping away from the bed. Before you can identify if it is a man or a woman, it disappears.

Everyone's mouths hang open.

Then the candles in the room light themselves. One of the visitors backs away and dashes down the closet stairs.

"Let me explain," says the guide.

She tells the story behind the hauntings. For a long time, this was a typical museum exhibit. Interesting, but certainly not paranormal. Then a family named Bruhns donated their grandmother's belongings. That's when strange things began to happen. The museum began repairing the newly refurbished colonial room.

Mrs. Bruhns was afraid her grandmother's portrait would be damaged during the typical confusion of a renovation. She wrapped it carefully then placed it in one of the dresser drawers. She laid it down next to her grandfather's Bible and firmly closed the drawer.

Finally, the renovation ended. Mrs. Bruhns retrieved her grandmother's picture. Wondering how it would look on the freshly polished dresser, she pulled off the protective wraps. Much to her surprise and disappointment, the glass frame had cracked in two places.

Later, Mrs. Bruhns explained the breakage by saying that her grandmother hadn't been pleased with the changes made to the exhibit. Breaking the glass was one way she could let people know she was angry.

Some of the visitors leave the tour, saying it was almost time for the museum to close. You and your grandmother are two of the few who choose to continue the tour.

When you step onto the Croghan-Schenley Ballroom, you're glad you stayed.

The ballroom, reconstructed so it looked as new as it did in the 1880s, took up two rooms of exhibit space.

"We think the hauntings originate with Mary Croghan. Her father dedicated the ballroom to her. Every curlicue, every carving, even the polished chandelier, were designed to make this the fanciest ballroom in Pittsburgh society. Mary, however, never made her debut."

Shortly after turning fifteen, she eloped with a man twenty-eight years older than she. What happened next? Did she die in an accident? Was there a tragedy that had taken place in the ballroom? Why was her ghost returning to the ballroom again and again?

The guide says that sometimes, ghost are drawn to places that hold strong emotion. Certainly, Mary Croghan knew she had ruined her father's hopes for her. Perhaps that's why she returns to the museum exhibit. Maybe she hopes to please her father by dancing in the ballroom, at last.

After the group files in, the guide shuts the exhibit door. The chandelier revolves, ever so slowly. The guide nods and says, "Thank you, Mary." She places a chair alongside the opposite wall. "This where it should stay. Mary likes to rearrange the furniture from time to time. However,

we at the museum want the ballroom to look just as it did in the 1800's.

"Time to go," says the guide. Your group squashes into an elevator. When it hits the thirteenth floor, it stops. The elevator door opens.

"Maybe another time," says the guide and pushes the button to close the door. "It's from the thirteenth floor where a professor jumped to his death. People say you can see his ghost on the ledge, just outside his office window."

The elevator door slides open on the first floor. You glance left, right, hoping for a last look at the spirits. None. For now. You will be back.

CHAPTER 10

The Ghosts of Saint Vincent College and Archabbey

You aren't happy. You're stuck in the backseat of the car, being nudged and poked by your big brother. He's touring colleges to find the best match. Today you're at Saint Vincent College in Latrobe, PA.

You know that the Pittsburgh Steelers run training camps at the school and hope you'll see some scrimmages. Even better, you've heard that Saint Vincent is full of ghosts. Maybe you'll see some.

You get your first chance to ghost hunt after your family leaves you alone. They want to sit in on your brother's appointment with an admissions dean. You don't. Everyone's pleased with the decision to let you wander alone around campus.

The Saint Vincent Grist Mill is on the top of your checklist of spirits. Not too many colleges have mills to grind wheat into flour, but Saint Vincent is no ordinary college. It's home to a monastery of Benedictine monks. Like most monasteries, Saint Vincent has to earn money to support the running of the monastery. The original monks were from Bavaria, a province in Germany known for its delicious bread.

Soon after their trip to Bavaria for recipes and instruction, the first monks here finished the mill and began providing flour to the locals.

Three stories tail, the mill is big enough to house several one-ton French quartz grinding stones. Locally mined coal provides energy to operate the steam engine that turns the stones. There's a massive arrangement of belts, pulleys and gears to guide the grain from the chutes to grinding stones. It's graceful and efficient. Except for when it's not.

One night a miller entangled himself in one of the belts and was crushed by the massive grinding stones.

You've heard that story before. Your brother loves to scare you. So does your dad. In fact, you remember many nights when your bedtime story included three-ton grinding stones.

You position yourself in front of a window in the grist mill store. The monks enjoy sharing the process of grinding grain, so have cut an observation window for people

to see the milling. Not only do the visitors get a first-hand lesson on making flour, they sometimes catch a glimpse of the poor miller. Apparently, he returns to the mill often. People says he's checking on the other millers, making sure they grind the grains correctly.

How do people know it is the unlucky monk that they see? You can't see the monk's face. A monk's hood can obscure eyes, nose and mouth into shadows. But can a shadow completely hide a face?

You wait and wait. No monk. Finally, you decide to come back later. You know that, in the past, the millers did their grinding at night. You'll wait for the faceless monk to return after dark.

Your brother is a fan of the paranormal, too. Two haunted dorms are at the top of his wish list for housing. You head to Aurelius Hall, his first choice.

You're surprised that no one stops you as you enter the hall. Maybe, you think, it's because it's visitors' day. It also helps that it's a scrimmage day for the Steelers. The dorm staff probably thinks you're a little lost brother who has gotten separated from his family. Part of that is true. You aren't with your parents and brother. But that was because you want to be alone. It's hard to ghost hunt when there are lots of people around.

You head to the seventh floor. That's where, a few years ago, a fire almost destroyed the top of the building. You've read that a freshman accidently started the fire. Some, though, think he tried to harness the flames to use them for a devil worship ceremony. Was he getting ready for a ritual when he had placed a circle of candles around himself? Somehow, he must have knocked a few over, for the wood floor ignited.

Luckily, although the fire was intense, it contained itself to the seventh floor.

Unluckily for the freshman, the smoke was intense, too. He died of smoke inhalation.

The next part of the story gives you the creeps. When a fireman found the boy, he almost turned to run away. The entire room was charred and burnt. Yet, the freshman's body was intact. Not a piece of ash or smudge of soot was found anywhere on his body.

Hoping the boy might still be alive, the fireman checked his pulse. In that space of a

few moments, the fireman burned his own hand. The boy's body was as hot as burning metal. The fireman called for help, and the crew decided to wait until the body was cool enough to be moved.

Strangely, this fire happened on April 29, the night before Walpurgis Day. Walpurgis Day is celebrated by Catholics all over the world. It's named for a female saint who battles sickness and surprisingly, witches. On the night before Walpurgis Day, witches are said to gather together. It is, people claim, the night to plan the next year's mayhem. Saint Walpurgis, it is said, counseled lighting bonfires to keep away the witches. Was the boy trying to protect the college against witches? Or was he trying to call them up to attack the college? No one knows.

The otherworldly fire might be gone, but paranormal activity stayed behind. Even though the seventh floor is no longer used for sleeping, it seems apparent that someone or something is still up there. Ever since that night, electronic devices flicker on and off and footsteps clomp on the floor above the dorms.

You slip into the stairwell and climb seven stories. You jiggle the door open. Maybe the monks are masters of grinding grain, but they have a lot to learn about security. The space is huge. Mountains of boxes lean this way and that. *Scritch, scrape, scritch*. What's that noise? Could it be the sound of matches being lit? Somewhere in front of you a pile of boxes leans. It tilts slowly, almost imperceptibly. Finally, it leans a degree too far. It tumbles to the floor. There's no chance the boxes could have hit you. You were out of the storage room and down a flight of stairs before the first one fell.

Once outside Aurelius Hall, you hear cheers and boos from the football stadium. The scrimmages are in play. You, however, have two more places to visit. Saint Benedict's Hall has a resident ghost. No devil worshipper or witch lives there. It's just a little girl named Jenny, too young for college or even boarding school. No one knows how and why she moved to Saint Benedict's Hall. Everyone does agree that she seems to like it there, for she's never left.

The dorm is almost empty. Everyone else must be watching the scrimmages. Aah, you sigh happily…uninterrupted surveillance. You stretch out on an empty bed. Nice of someone to make it for you, you think. You look up to the ceiling and listen. There's a rush of thumps on the floor above, followed by a stream of giggles. The pattern repeats itself. After a while, the noise is no longer startling, it's almost hypnotic. After a while, you fall asleep. It's been a long day. The predawn car trip, the frenzied search for last minute forms and applications and the running up and down dorm stairs, that's enough to make any kid want a nap.

"What are you doing in my bed?"

Opening your eyes, you see a six-foot-tall boy standing over you. He doesn't seem angry. He seems confused. "What are you doing there?" he repeats

"I was looking for Jenny," you say. "Then I got tired. I tried to take a little rest."

The boy hoots. "Looking for the ghost girl? You must not have tried very hard." He points to a window. "See?"

You're on the fifth floor, high enough to guarantee injuries or death if you fall. The glass is dirty. You can't see anything. The smears make it hard to see .

The boy laughs again. "Look at the smudges again."

There were marks on the window, but not the kind made by greasy pizza hands. These are little handprints, small enough to be made by a child. You walk over and squat down to investigate.

You're not sure if the handprints belong to a girl or a boy. But you're certain about their placement. The handprints have been made by someone who was outside the dorm, five stories up.

The roar from the stadium makes you run to another window.

"They'll be finished soon," says the young man. "You'd better go if you want to see any of it."

He walks you down the stairs. "If you really like ghosts, have your parents bring you here on Founder's Day. That's when the school's founder, Boniface Wimmer, rises from his grave."

He must have noticed your face, which had changed from the pink of embarrassment to the white of fright.

"Oh, I see you're not anxious to see that," he says. "It's not scary. Boniface Wimmer loved this school. He wanted it to be the best education for miles around. So, they say, on the anniversary of Saint Vincent's founding, he leaves his grave behind and walks the campus. He stops at this place or that, checking to see if everything is running smoothly. Some say he only uses red doors, which makes sense, in a way."

"Why?" you ask.

"The last red door he enters is the one that leads to the crypts. There he offers prayers for the people who died before he could bless them."

Hmm. You wonder. He might be a kind priest, but he was still a dead one. You'd like to postpone that meeting until you're completely prepared. An ectoplasm trap? Particle thrower? Ectoplasmic glasses? That might take some time to collect. You'll wait.

Conclusion

Have you picked your favorite haunting spot? Is it a secluded dark road? It might be a ghostly house or a town of spooks. Could it be a grain mill, a university or one of the many museums that house unsettled spirits? Southwestern Pennsylvania has so many ghosts that a two-week road trip won't be enough time to see them all. So, save this guide for the next time you want a good, old-fashioned scare. It won't disappoint!

Karen Emily Miller has been writing about strange creatures since she was six, so writing about the paranormal is a perfect fit. She just moved to Iowa City and is excited to meet the ghosts who live there.

Check out some of the other Spooky America titles available now!

Spooky America was adapted from the creeptastic Haunted America series for adults. Haunted America explores historical haunts in cities and regions across America. Each book chronicles both the widely known and less-familiar history behind local ghosts and other unexplained mysteries. Here's more from *Ghosts of Southwestern Pennsylvania* author Thomas White:

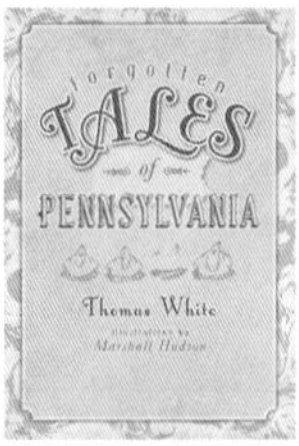